Mom, Can I Have a Dragon?

To Hana

Take Care
of George!

T.E. Watson

By T.E. Watson
Illustrated by Dave Patterson

To Kyle Z. from Grandaddy.

This book is for all the wee beasties I could not bring home when I wanted to.
And for Little, the best cat and animal friend I have ever known.

Thanks!
T. E. Watson

Text / Story and concept Copyright © 2002 Author T. E. Watson (Thomas E. Watson)
Illustrations are copyright © 2003 Dave Patterson
Cover Design: Dave Patterson, Tom Watson, René Schmidt
Layout, Design Editor: René Schmidt
Publisher: Paw Prints Press LLC, an imprint of Highlander Celtic Publications

"Mom, Can I Have A Dragon?" ISBN 1-58478-020-7
Library of Congress Cataloging-in-Publication Data
Library of Congress Control Number (LCCN) 2001012345
T.E. Watson - Author
Mom, Can I Have A Dragon? - Fictional story picture book for children.
Reading level - 7–12 years
Summary - Sam brings home a strange unexpected new pet that he hopes to convince his parents to add to the family.
Additional subjects - pets, dragons, juvenile action, family issues, family communication, responsibility.
Case Bound, Pages 32, Full color, Smythe sewn.
Printed in Hong Kong. Second Printing

Sam was excited!

The back porch screen door slammed behind him as he clomped up the hallway from the kitchen to the base of the stairs and called out.

"Mom? Are you home?"

No answer. Sam called again. "Mom?"

Mom came to the top of the stairs, with rubber gloves and a scrub brush. Wiping her forehead with her sleeve, she asked, "Samuel, what is it?"

"Mom, can I have a dragon?"

Mother corrected him. "May I have a dragon?"

"May I have a dragon?" Sam asked.

"No, you may not have a dragon." She answered, as if she really believed Sam, but gave him an odd look just the same. "Dinner will be in half an hour, so get washed up."

Disappointed, Sam said, "All right." He hung his head and scuffed his feet as he walked to the back porch door.

Sam went outside and looked up.

"Mom said I can't keep you. But you wait; you'll grow on her. She's not so bad for a mom."

Standing in front of Sam was a large green and red, winged dragon. Not the scary fire breathing sort, this dragon was friendly. He had kind eyes and a long tail and sounded a bit like a cat's purring.

Sam took off the rope leash he had made to bring his new large friend home and asked him, "Where am I going to put you until Mom and Dad say I can keep you?"

They walked over to the old doghouse. Sam looked at the doghouse, and then looked up at the dragon. Sam looked at the doghouse once more and then looked up again. They both looked at each other with their heads shaking "no".

"Nope! Where am I going to keep you? I know. The storm cellar!"

Sam guided his newfound friend to the cellar, lifted the large cellar doors, and they both walked quietly down the stairs to the hiding place.

The cellar was perfect. It was dark, cool, a little damp, and there was plenty of room for a dragon. The dragon settled into a corner that suited him just right. The best thing about the cellar was that nobody ever went down there.

"Hey, wait a minute." Sam thought for a second. "You need a name. I know! How about "George"? There was a dragon in history named George, I think. What do you think? Do you like the name?"

George nodded his huge head in agreement with a large dragon grin.

"Well, then, George it is."

Dinnertime came and Sam heard his mom calling him to come eat.

"Oh, I forgot to get you something to eat!" Sam said. "What do dragons eat? Maybe there will be some leftovers? I will come back with some food for you. Do you like salad? We always have lots of salad. Do you like dressing?"

George shrugged his shoulders, not knowing for sure if he did.

"Okay, I will be back after dinner with some salad. You get comfortable."

Sam ran up to dinner. He washed his hands and sat down, showed mom his hands and dug in.

"Hey, slow down, Son. You're going to make yourself sick eating that fast." Sam's father said.

"Have some salad?" Mom asked.

Sam's little sister Emily sat in her highchair and played with her peas, smashing them into her mouth.

Sam replied, through a mouthful of food, "Yes, please."

Mom dished out the portion that Sam normally ate.

"Can I..." Sam corrected himself. "May I have more than that, Mom?"

"More? Are you sure you can eat all that?" she asked.

Sam was chewing as fast as he could, and answered, "Yes."

"Do you want any dressing?"

"NO!" Sam answered, losing a bit of what he was chewing. "Excuse me," said Sam, regaining his manners. "No, thank you. Dragons don't like dressing."

Mom looked at Sam oddly. "All right."

Sam continued to chow down all he could eat and was soon finished.

"Dad, I have homework, could I bring the rest up to my room? I'll eat it there."

Sam refilled his plate with a large pile of salad. Now, both parents looked at him, wondering why their boy was so hungry.

Sam pushed his chair back and took the plate of dragon dinner.

Sam went down the hallway, he quietly went out the front door, tiptoed down the front steps, and finally made his way around to the cellar with George's dinner.

"Here you go, George. I made sure it doesn't have any dressing."

George gently reached out and took the plate of greens and held it up to eat.

A satisfied deep purring sound came from George as he ate. Munch, munch, munch. He was a happy dragon.

Sam said, "Hey, don't eat so fast. You'll get a stomachache."

Before Sam knew it, George was done and settling in for bedtime.

Sam sat next to George and held his paw until his large friend fell deeply and peacefully asleep. Sam knew he had to do his homework, so he quietly got up, careful not to wake George, and went upstairs to his room.

Bedtime soon came to the household. It was a beautiful night. The stars shined, the moon glowed, and only the sound of a smooth breeze rustling through the trees could be heard, until a strange deep purring sounded through the floor vents.

The purring became deeper in tone, so deep the sound began to vibrate through the walls. The vibration grew loud enough to wake Sam and his parents.

Sam's mom awoke with a start. "Oh, my goodness! Honey, wake up. The house is falling apart!"

Sam's dad fell out of bed and stumbled to his bathrobe.

"What in the world?"

"Sam, Sam? Are you all right?" Dad called out. "Check the baby!"

Sam was already downstairs in the cellar. He knew the noise was George purring soundly. But how do you wake a dragon? Especially one as large as George?

"George," Sam whispered loudly. "George, George. Wake up, George. George, shhhhh. George, please be quiet." Sam pleaded. "Mom and Dad are going to find you. Now they are never going to let me keep you."

Sam tried pulling George's tail, tugging his big toe, and even tried to hold the dragon's very large nose to keep him from purring.

It was too late. There, standing in the cellar doorway, was Mom and Dad, being led by the beam of a flashlight with Dad holding baby Emily, who was still sound asleep.

They stood there with their mouths gaping wide open. Mom was about to scream in fright when Sam reminded her, "Mom, don't! You'll wake him."

Mom covered her mouth with her hand to keep quiet and sat down with a plop on the cellar steps. Sam's parents could not believe their eyes.

Sam knew he was in trouble. George was waking up, first smacking his mouth, then opening one eye and then the next. Then he sat up as much as he could, having much the same reaction that Sam's parents did.

"Mom, I asked you if I could have a dragon. His name is George and he won't be a problem. I will take care of him, and he doesn't need to be paper-trained. And all he eats is salad," Sam told them.

Sam's parents looked at each other at the mention of salad.

George was a little frightened. Sam held his front paw to help him calm down.

Sam's father took off his glasses to clean them, just to make sure he was not seeing things. Placing them back on his face, he scratched his head in amazement.

"Samuel, where in the world did you find a dragon? What do you think you are going to do with him?"

"But, Dad," Sam pleaded. "I found him wandering in the cow field next to my school. He was eating some hay. He didn't look like he belonged to anyone so I brought him home."

"What are you going to do with him when we go to the company picnic on Saturday? You had better think of something. We don't have room to keep a dragon," Dad said.

George knew that tone of voice. He'd heard it before at the house he had to leave behind when the people made him go. A large dragon tear rolled down his green cheek. He hoped he wouldn't have to go. George liked Sam and George liked the cellar, it felt comfortable to him and he wished he would be able to stay. This was the best home he ever had. Sam was sad, too. He had to figure out what to do with George so his parents would let him stay.

The next morning all was quiet again. Sam got up early to feed George.

"Good morning, big fella. Here's some breakfast. More salad?"

Sam watched as George ate his breakfast and finished what was left of last night's greens.

"George, I have to go to school now. I will be back in a few hours. You will be okay in the cellar. You have to be quiet and don't let Mom hear you. Maybe she'll think you were a dream and forget about last night, at least until I get home." Sam crossed his fingers and walked George to the back of the cellar to his comfy corner, gave him a big hug and went back to his room to get ready for school.

Sam came clomping down the stairs with his bookpack in tow. Mom, Dad and Emily were at the table already eating breakfast.

"I had the strangest dream last night. It seemed so real," Dad said.

Mom replied, "Yeah, so did I."

Sam didn't say anything. He pretended as if he didn't hear a word they said.

"Dad, would you drive me to school today?" Sam asked. "I have a bunch of heavy books from homework."

Drinking a last sip of coffee, Dad said, "Sure, Son. Let me get my briefcase."

Mom went about her morning routine, taking care of Emily, never thinking about what had happened the night before.

For Sam, the school day seemed to go on forever. All he could think of was if Mom was going to find George.

The recess bell rang and Sam's class went outside to play. Ben, Sam's best friend, ran up to him and asked, "Are you okay?"

"Ben, you are my best friend, right? And I can trust you?"

Ben answered, "Yeah."

Sam said, "You can't tell anyone else about this. You have to promise."

Ben became curious.

"Okay, okay, what is it?"

"I have a dragon in my cellar."

Ben crossed his arms in disbelief and raised an eyebrow. "Yeah, right."

"You have to believe me," Sam said. "He really is in my cellar. You come to my house after school and I'll show you."

When the final bell rang, the boys ran all the way to Sam's house and straight to the storm cellar.

Breathless, Sam said, "We have to be quiet. He is probably asleep and we don't want to scare him." The boys quietly went down the steps.

"He's over there in the corner. George, it's me. I'm home. I brought a friend. Ben, it's okay, come on over."

George was very glad to see Sam and greeted them both with a big toothy dragon grin.

Ben was caught completely by surprise.

"Wow! Cool! Where did you get him?"

Sam began to explain, "I found him next to the school yesterday. He was eating hay from the bales in the field. He didn't look like he had a home so I brought him here to the cellar. George wants to stay and I want him to stay, and Mom and Dad don't really know he is here yet. You have any ideas?"

Ben was stumped. He did not have a single clue how Sam could keep George. Sam became more worried. He wanted to keep George so much. He had to find a way. But how?

Saturday morning arrived. Sam got up earlier than the rest of the family and went to the kitchen. He gathered up all the leftover salad makings he could, not touching the salad Mom made for the picnic so he wouldn't draw suspicion. He took the big pile of greens to George for his breakfast.

"My family is going to a company picnic today. We won't be back until dark. You will be all right by yourself. You take care of the house. George, don't you worry. I'll find a way for you to stay."

Sam hugged George's large neck, patted his head, and then left for the picnic with his family.

George slept the day away. Night fell and it was getting later. George was wondering where Sam was, and decided to take a look for himself. With a push of his huge head, George opened the cellar doors. He looked from side to side to see if the coast was clear to come out.

But then he heard some strange crashing noises coming from inside the house. George knew it wasn't Sam. He wasn't home yet. George remembered that Sam asked him to take care of the house while the family was gone for the day. So George went out to investigate.

George went to the kitchen window first. He looked inside, but didn't see anything.

Then he quietly went to the side of the house and peered into the family room window. Nothing in there either. But when he headed back for the cellar, George heard a crash come from upstairs.

George sat up, stretched his long neck, and looked inside an upstairs hallway window.

There, he saw a scruffy man dressed in black with a mask, and carrying a large pillowcase. He was filling it with the family's belongings. He even took Sam's prized baseball cards.

George knew that he couldn't let this thief take the family's things, so he watched silently and waited for the burglar to leave the house. George watched this sneaky thief go from room to room until finally the robber went downstairs to the kitchen, and began to put all the silverware and plates in his bag.

George crouched down, and with his eyes just surfacing over the windowsill, saw what the crook was stealing.

The burglar was taking George's special salad plate.

This was the last straw!

George mustered up all the courage he could, all the way from the tip of his tail to the end of his big dragon snout. As quiet as a mouse, George waited in the darkness of the back yard.

The burglar quietly closed the back door as he came out, and started to sneak off across the yard.

But before he could get halfway, George rose up, growled his best dragon growl, and spread his wings all the way out.

The thief screamed in fright,
and George brought his huge
tail down on top of him.

The burglar did not know
what hit him!

The burglar struggled to escape from George's giant tail, but George did not let him budge. George kept him there and faithfully waited for the family to come home.

A short while passed, and George's ears perked up when he heard the family car pull into the drive.

As they entered the house they heard cries for help coming from the backyard.

"Help! Get me out of here!"

Everyone ran through the house to the back porch to see what the emergency was.

Dad switched on the yard lights and there, still standing guard over the burglar who was still holding the bag of stolen loot, was George with a very pleased dragon smile.

George did not care that Sam's parents found him now. He had stopped this scoundrel from taking the family's things.

"Look, Dad," Sam said in all the excitement. "George caught a burglar!"

Dad said in disbelief, "You mean this is a real dragon? We weren't dreaming?"

Mom was trying to hold Emily, who was reaching out to touch George, when Emily spoke her first word. "Duppy?"

Mom forgot all about what was happening. "Did you hear that? Emily spoke!"

Sam had to think fast.

"Dad, you said if I could think of what I was going to do with George, I could keep him. It seems to me he has done that for us. George can be our guard dragon! HE did save all our stuff. Please!"

Emily became more excited and reached out again to touch George. "Big Duppy!"

Mom realized that George was really there and that the burglar had been stopped from taking all the family's belongings. She thought for a moment and smiled at George.

"With Emily talking and since she likes this big moose, and with George catching burglars and protecting the house, it might not be so bad having a dragon as part of the family. Sam, if your dad agrees, you may keep him," she said.

Sam looked at his dad. "Please, please, *ple-e-ease?*"

"You heard your mom. If it's all right with her then it's fine with me, but you must take care of him."

Dad called the police and they soon arrived. The burglar was put in the squad car and was on his way to jail.

On the way to the precinct, the officers thought how they were going to explain this in their report.

"Did you see that?"

"Nope, didn't see a thing."

"That's what I thought."

And they continued on.

The night's events came to a close and everything settled back to normal... sort of.

Mom, Dad, and Emily were sound asleep in their beds.

And in the basement, Sam and George were snugly curled up and dreaming of all the great days they would have together.

To Be Continued......

T. E. Watson in Nairn, Scotland.

T.E. Watson is the award winning children's author of 63 books, including his very popular *I Wanna Iguana*, *The Monster In The Mailbox*, and *Glen Robbie/A Scottish Fairy Tale*, one of a series of 6 original Celtic Children's Stories. He is also the author/ columnist of the successful serialized tale for children *The Feather River Adventure*. To have him visit your school please contact him at tew@tewatsononline.com.

Dave Patterson lives in McMinnville, Oregon with his wife Carla and a couple of Westie Terriers.

This is his first published book.

Dave's artwork can also be seen online at www.davepattersonart.com.